Annick Press

Toronto   New York   Vancouver

The Magic Mustache

by Gary Barwin

illustrated by Stéphane Jorisch

Annick Press Ltd.

We acknowledge the support of the Canada Council for the Arts for our publishing program. We also thank the Ontario Arts Council.

We acknowledge the financial support of the Government of Canada through the Book Publishing Industry Development Program for our publishing activities.

Cataloguing in Publication Data

Barwin, Gary
        The magic mustache

ISBN 1-55037-607-1 (bound)
ISBN 1-55037-606-3 (pbk.)

I. Jorisch, Stéphane. II Title

PS8553.A783M33 1999   jC813'.54
C99-930302-3 PZ7.B28585Ma 1999

The art in this book was rendered in water color, gouache, and pen and ink. The text was type-set in Base 9.

Distributed in Canada by:
Firefly Books Ltd.
3680 Victoria Park Avenue
Willowdale, ON
M2H 3K1

Published in the USA by:
Annick Press (U.S.) Ltd.

Distributed in the USA by:
Firefly Books (U.S.) Inc.
P.O. Box 1338
Ellicott Station
Buffalo, NY 14205

Printed and bound in Canada by:
Friesens, Altona, Manitoba.

For my three noses —
full of (magic) beans
G. B.

For my three mouths
I feed every day
S. J.

There once was a nose

who lived with his two old parents, who were both eyes. The family was very poor and had nothing but a pair of glasses that the eyes had been given as a wedding present.

One day the mother eye said to the father eye, "We have no more food. Our nose must go to the market and trade our glasses for something to eat."

On the way to market, the nose met an old ear and her husband, who offered to trade the pair of glasses for a mustache.

"But why would I trade these beautiful glasses for a plain old mustache?" the nose asked. "In a few years I'll be able to grow one of my own."

"Because," the old woman ear said, "this is a magic mustache."

"It is?" the nose said.

"So we've heard," the husband ear said.

The nose thought he smelled luck in the air, and so he agreed to the trade.

When the nose showed his parents the mustache, the two old eyes were angry with him for making such a worthless trade.

"Now we have nothing but our tears," they cried.

They threw the mustache out the window and then they all went to bed. Hungry.

The next morning the nose saw that the mustache had indeed been magic. It had grown into a huge and bushy beard that reached far into the sky.

"Good morning!" the beard said.
"what!?" said the surprised nose.

"I said good morning!"

"I've never heard of a talking beard before," the nose said.

"Well, you noses don't often listen. You usually look down on us beards," the beard said. "But not that nose named Jack — he listened."

"Who?" the nose asked.

"Jack," the beard said. "Surely you've heard
the story about Jack and the beard talk,"
the beard giggled. "Now climb me," it said.

And the nose did.

At the top of the beard, the nose found himself
at the castle of a giant **mouth**.

The nose was in the kitchen looking for food when the giant mouth returned home, burst through the door and stomped around the castle, shouting:

Nose Pie
1 Large Nose

Macaroni & Nose

"Fee fi fum foes,
I smell a nose.
Be it **big** or be it small,
If that nose doesn't beat it,
This mouth is going to eat *it*!"

The nose hid in a suit of armor. But the mouth soon became too tired to look for the nose, brushed his teeth with a golden toothbrush, and fell into a deep sleep.

The nose tiptoed over, grabbed the golden toothbrush, dropped it down the beard, and climbed after it. Then the nose cut down the beard with a **big scissors.**

"Hey! What are you doing?" the beard protested.

"It's just a trim," the nose said. "You'll grow again."

The next morning the nose saw that
the beard had indeed grown *huge* and bushy.

"I told you that you'd grow,"
the nose said to the beard.

"It was a lot of work," the beard said.
"I hope you appreciate it. Now climb me again."

The nose was again looking for food when the giant mouth returned home and clomped around, yelling:

"Fee fi fo feard,
A nose has appeared up a giant beard.
Be it **big** or be it small,
After he's chased it,
This mouth is going to taste it!"

The nose hid behind a football. But the mouth soon became very thirsty and took out his magic straw. You only had to sip from this straw – you didn't even need a glass – and all day you could taste your favorite drink. The giant mouth had a sip and in no time fell fast asleep.

The nose snatched the magic straw, dropped it down to the ground, then climbed after it. Again the nose snipped down the beard.

"You've got your work cut out for you," the nose said.

"Here we grow again," the beard said.

By the following morning the beard reached back up into the sky.

"I don't think I can keep doing this," the beard said.

"Hair today, gone tomorrow."

The nose climbed up to the castle. Again the mouth burst through the door and stamped around, bellowing:

"Fee fi fo something,
I'm really mad & nose,
I'll tell you one thing:
Be you **big** or be you small,
If I find you,
My teeth are going to grind you!"

The nose hid under a handkerchief. But the mouth soon felt sleepy and lay down on his bed.

"Play me something really bad," the mouth ordered, and his magic harmonica said, "Yes, my Master Mouth," and began to play a horrible lullaby.

As soon as the mouth was asleep, the nose grabbed the magic harmonica and ran toward the door.

But the harmonica called out,

"Help, Master Mouth, I'm being stolen by a nose!" The giant mouth woke up roaring, and chased after the nose. The nose got to the top of the beard first.

The nose dropped the magic harmonica
down to the ground, then quickly climbed
after it. The mouth was close behind him,
gnashing his giant teeth.

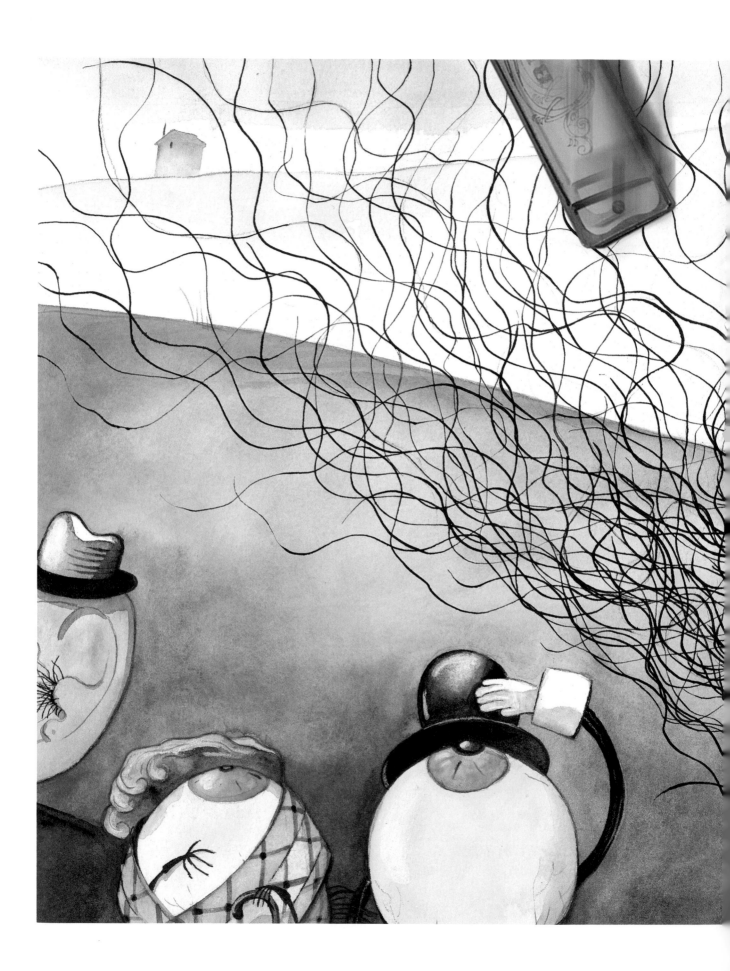

The nose's parents, the eyes, were watching from the bottom of the beard. The old ear and her husband were also there, listening. And the nose was ahead by, well, only a nose.

"This is hair-raising," the beard laughed, shaking so hard that the nose and the giant mouth slipped and fell to the ground with a horrible **crash**.

When the dust had finally settled, the magic harmonica could see that the beard, the giant mouth and the nose, together with the two eyes and the old ears, had made a face. And if you've ever made a face, perhaps you were warned that it might stay that way, which is **exactly** what happened to this face. It stayed that way, happily **ever after.**

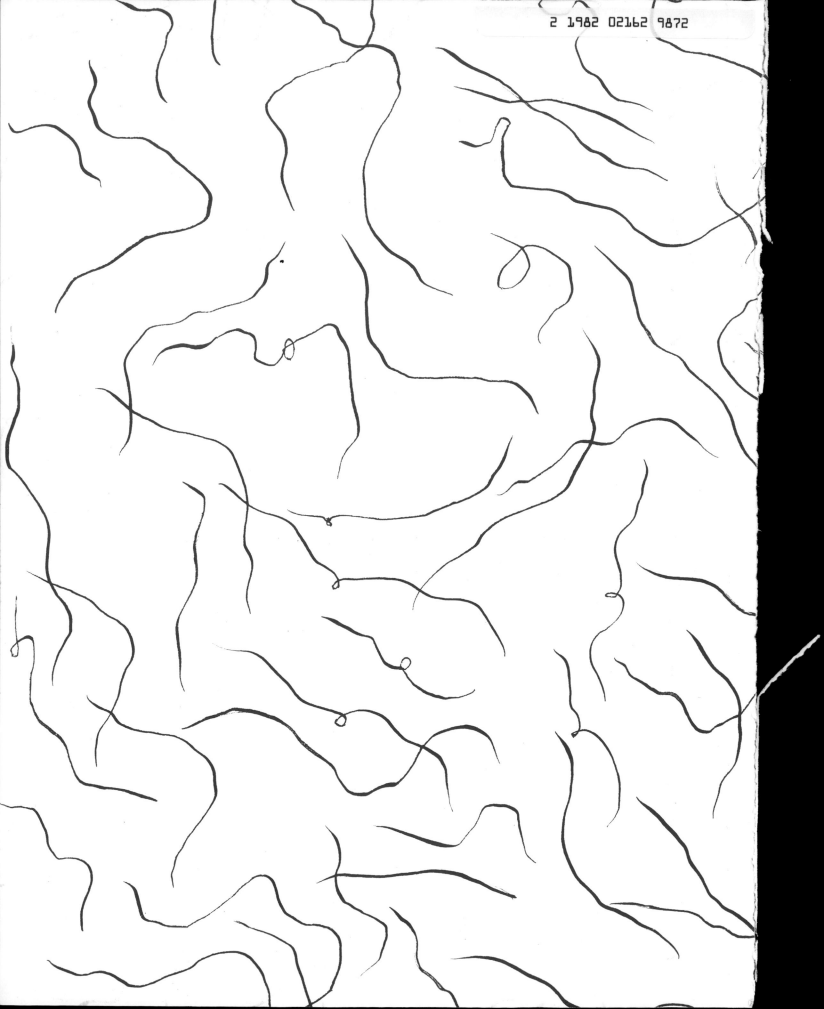